LEAH'S STAR

MARGARET BATESON-HILL
& KARIN LITTLEWOOD

Alanna Max

Bethlehem was always a busy city. Tonight it was more crowded than ever. The Roman emperor Augustus had ordered a census, so everyone who had been born in the city had returned to be registered.

Leah's father had sent her for more food. The guests staying at his inn were hungry. But she was struggling to get through the crowds.

Leah finally reached her own street. But suddenly,
she stopped quite still. A great silver star was
shining right above her home. It was so beautiful
that she could only gaze upwards, amazed by its
shining splendour...

Leah didn't see the donkey until she felt a sharp kick on her knee! A man called, "Look out!" just as her father came running out from the inn.

"What took you so long?" he asked. "Pick everything up, then come and help. I'm rushed off my feet."

Leah wiped her tears away on her sleeve. Her knee and her feelings hurt. A strong pair of arms lifted her back onto her feet. The man was leading a woman sitting on the donkey. She was young and very pregnant.

As Leah picked up the vegetables, she heard the woman say, "Joseph, the baby is coming! What are we going to do?"

Leah looked over to her father who nodded in understanding.

"There's no room in my inn," he said, "but I've got a stable. It's not much, but it's warm and dry, and quiet."

Leah's father told her to show the couple to the stable and as Leah took the donkey's reins, she heard him call across the street to Susanna to come and help.

After the coldness and dark outside, the stable was warm and comforting. Susanna immediately took charge. "Leah, get another light and some blankets for Mary."

Leah helped as best she could. Suddenly, she realized there was no cradle, so she filled the animals' feed box with new hay and covered it with a blanket of her own.

Susanna walked around the stable with Mary. "Just take things slowly," she advised. "It could be a long night."

Leah found a corner and lay down. She realised she could still see the star. It glowed brightly, as though it were watching over the stable.

As she lay in the warm, sweet-smelling hay, her thoughts began to drift. With Susanna's help, Mary would soon be a mother! She wondered if her own mother ever watched over her from somewhere high above…

Leah didn't wake until she heard a cry.

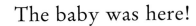

The baby was here!

Leah crept slowly out of her dark corner.
Mary was cradling her newborn son with such
love and tenderness that Leah suddenly felt shy.

Then Susanna caught sight of her and laughed.

"What happened to my little helper? Come and
see the new baby. His name is Jesus."

Leah could only gaze in wonder. The baby was so
tiny and perfect, snuggled in his mother's arms that
she wanted to cry!

Then there was a quiet knock.
It was Leah's father, looking puzzled.
"There are some shepherds outside
and they want to see the baby."
  Slowly the shepherds crowded in.
Their faces mirrored the long, hard
seasons spent in the open, but their
eyes shone with a fierce joy. The
oldest one spoke in a trembling voice.
  "We saw bright angels in the night
sky. They told us about the baby; that
he was the Christ, the king we have
been waiting for."

Leah stared at the shepherd in disbelief.
"Jesus was a king? Then why wasn't
he born in a palace?"

Was Jesus really a special baby?
Leah could think of nothing else.
Finally, she just had to ask Mary.

"Every baby is special," Mary replied, "but I believe that
Jesus is the chosen one of God. And I believe that God will
look after him, just as he did by bringing us to your stable.
"Of course, he couldn't have done that without you, Leah."

"Me?" said Leah.
Mary smiled. "God often chooses little people
to do great things for him."

That night, the star was shining so brightly Leah thought the whole world must know that Jesus was in her stable.

She crept to the window to catch one last glimpse but found herself looking at three travellers, richly dressed in silken robes.

Leah ran to open the inn door.
One of the travellers bent down
to her and she could smell the
perfume of the oils that scented his
skin. The sound of his voice made
her think of faraway places.

"We are scholars. We have
followed the star for many days.
But it shines above a stable. Tell us
we have not journeyed in vain.
Is the Christ child within?"

"Yes," whispered Leah, "he's here."

The travellers entered the stable and
when they saw the baby and his
mother, they fell to their knees. They
brought out gold, frankincense and
myrrh - gifts fit for a king.

"But if you have followed
the star," thought Leah,
"who else will be coming…"

Leah woke up just before dawn. She knew at once
that the silver star was gone. But had Jesus gone too?
Leah ran to the stable and softly pushed open the door.

Everything had been tidied away but Mary, Joseph and the baby were still there! "Are you going away?" she whispered.

"Yes," Mary sighed, "Joseph had a dream... the King's soldiers are coming."

Mary turned to Leah with a sad, gentle smile and asked her to hold the baby while she got ready. Leah knew this was goodbye.

She sat quietly, and treasured everything about the baby – his silky hair, his soft, dark skin, his watchful eyes.

But when his tiny fingers clasped one of her own, she had the strangest feeling that it was not her holding the baby, but the baby holding her…

🐾 Alanna Max

This hardback edition published in 2019 by
Alanna Max
38 Oakfield Road
London N4 4NL
www.alannamax.com
Under licence from 2AM

First published as *Leah's Christmas Story*
By Lion Children's Books in 2006
Under licence from 2AM

HB1
Printed in China

ISBN: 978-1-907825-255